SEATTLE PUBLIC LIBRARY

THIS IS NO LONGER THE PROPERTY
OF THE SEATTLE PUBLIC LIBRARY

Colors Come from God . . . Just Like Me!

CAROLYN A. FORCHÉ

ILLUSTRATED BY CHARLES COX

Text Copyright © 1995 by Carolyn A. Forché
Illustrations Copyright © 1995 by Abingdon Press
All rights reserved
Printed in Hong Kong

96 97 98 99 00 01 02 03 04 — 10 9 8 7 6 5 4 3 2

Abingdon Press/Nashville

For my granddaughter, Chelsea . . .
My beautiful, brown princess.

Acknowledgments

COLORS COME FROM GOD . . . JUST LIKE ME!

I must first give thanks to God for moving upon my spirit to write this book. I had no thought of publishing this story. However, in God's divine plan for children, He put two wonderful people in my life. Jerry and Janet Weiner, both published authors and former professors of journalism, happened by chance to see my story and insisted that I enter it as a submission for the 1994 Manuscriptors Guild's Annual Guilded Quill Award. Because of their encouragement, COLORS COME FROM GOD . . . JUST LIKE ME was awarded 2nd Place for Children's Books that year. To Janet and Jerry, I am ever grateful. Your eye for potential will now help children the world over to see their own potential in a significant way in this book.

To my daughter Lisa and her husband, Reginald McCoy, I thank you both for giving me Chelsea, without whom the passion for this book would not have been inspired. To my son, Laird, thank you for your constant nudgings to "Just do it, Mom!" I thank my late parents, Larney L. Sr., and Hester Simmons Johnson, who showed me by their own example that love knows no color.

Finally, to Chelsea, my little princess, thank you for those special words of love you gave me when I needed to feel your inner love expressed . . . the most memorable of which was your response when I said, "I betcha' I love you more than you love me." And you said back to me:

"N-o-o-o, I love you more than you love me, because I loved you before I was even even born . . . and because I knew I was coming, I loved you first, so that means I love you more!"

Introduction

The words pierced my heart like poison darts . . . "I don't want to be brown anymore!"

This summarily determined statement was coming from my daughter's daughter; a little girl whose room was filled with beautiful brown dolls, books about pretty little chocolate brown, tan, and ebony-hued children, as well as a balanced array of other children's books showing the multi-cultural and multi-colored faces all around us."Who could have hurt my 'little Ethiopian princess'—as I often addressed her, I wondered? What could they have done or said to hurt her so?"

This book is dedicated to all children. For all children at one time or another suffer the slings and arrows of hurtful, alienating words that say: "You're different. You're unacceptable because . . ." Sadly, we have too often taught children that human beings are to be valued or invalidated largely on physical attributes.

This poetic telling, though written to my granddaughter, healed the child in me first! My prayer is that it will be a balm to my beloved Chelsea, her children, and all the children of the world. They must be completely convinced of God's special love in creating them as they are. And we must consistently reassure children that those who hurt them with words, attitudes, mistreatment and cold stares must be forgiven, prayed for, and ultimately healed of strife and offense themselves—so that God's rainbow of colors may come full circle.

Carolyn Forché

Foreword

One of the joys of my life is the privilege to speak before many children in schools, churches, and community settings. I cherish the opportunity to encourage and motivate children to achieve the potential that is theirs. All too often I meet sad and discouraged faces of children who ask me things much too painful or sensitive to commit to writing here; but their bruised sense of esteem is often bottom-lined in the question: "Why did I have to be born this way?" I wish I had a copy of this book for all the children I meet every week to instill in them the belief in their special gift of uniqueness given by God.

My parents not only shared the limitless possibilities of achievement through biblical principles, as does COLORS COME FROM GOD . . . JUST LIKE ME, but also ingrained in me the knowledge that no one could consider himself or herself better than I am as a human being unless I allowed it. I believe this story will be a stepping-stone for all children who at one point in their young lives will say and feel, "Why me?" It is a book that will go much further, in a significant way, in molding their self concepts than the unattainable heroes and heroines of today's heavily-hyped animated films, or the outdated nursery-rhyme concepts of "sugar and spice and everything nice."

Robert Reid
Former star of the Houston Rockets
Currently Program Executive of
Community Outreach,
Houston Astros

*The Bible says
God spoke a word,
And all things came to be!
There were fish, birds, the sea, and stars,

*Then God made kids like me!

**Genesis Chapter 1*
**Acts 17:26*

*The Bible says that God made us
from dust upon the ground;
And God made me a beautiful brown!

**Genesis 2:7*

*God placed us in a garden,
full of colors and lots of sun,
And God kept this garden watered
with four rivers in Africa.

**Genesis 2:10-14*

*God made the sun that shines above,
so yellow, gold, and bright;
God made the moon the whitest white
to lighten up the night.

**Genesis 1:14-18*

*God made trees so tall and strong,
Grow green straight from the ground,
And God made me a beautiful brown!

**Genesis 1:11-12*

*God made the sky a pretty pastel blue,
And God made the rainbow,
His promised gift come true.

*Genesis 1:8
*Genesis 9:13-17

*God made fat green frogs
That make a funny sound,
And God made me
a beautiful brown!

Genesis 1:25

*God colored yummy, juicy apples
red, green, and yellow.
God made berries sweetest
when they are dark and mellow.

**Genesis 1:11*

*God made my goldfish
that swim 'round and 'round,
And God made me
a beautiful brown.

**Genesis 1:20-21*

God made butterflies
every color we can name;
Though it's hard to catch them,
It's fun trying just the same.

God made the cockatoo
who sports a yellow crown;
And God made me
a beautiful brown!

God made the honeybees
make honey as they do.
God made the eggplant
a dark purple hue.

God made the busy ants
that build their homes in mounds;
And God made me
a beautiful brown!

*The Bible says when God made us,
He made us in His image;
That simply means,
When God sees us,
He sees in us His goodness.

**Genesis 1:27*

God made many kinds of people,
some short, some thin, some tall.
We see them in their cars, in school,
and by hundreds in the malls.

Sometimes people misbehave;
They say some hurtful things.
We pray God's love will fill their hearts,
And let them see their shame.

Of all the things that God made good,
None are better than you;
God made you extra special
When God made you!

God has planted a garden of
the children He has made;
Blossoms red, blossoms brown,
yellow, black, and white;
And God wants us to grow together
in His truth and light.

Because we're planted in His heart,
and rooted in His love;
We thirst for heavenly showers
which He feeds us from above.

Whatever color God chose for you,
It pleases Him very much,
And God wants you to see yourself—
A child His love has touched.

Aren't you glad God made you special?
No one is exactly like you,
And we make God especially happy
in good things we say and do.

God has made a big round world
of many kids a lot like me,
from faraway places,
with different-looking faces,
A rainbow of children are we.

But I'm really very glad,
When God looked the world around,
deciding just who I would be.
I imagine He said,
"Hum-m-m-m-m-m-m,
now let me see—"

And God made me a beautiful brown!